Infinite Intruder

Infinite Intruder

by Alan E. Nourse

It was the second time they tried that Roger Strang realized someone was trying to kill his son.

The first time there had been no particular question. Accidents happen. Even in those days, with all the Base safety regulations and strict speed-way lane laws, young boys would occasionally try to gun their monowheels out of the slow lanes into the terribly swift traffic; when they did, accidents did occur. The first time, when they brought David home in the Base ambulance, shaken but unhurt, with the twisted smashed remains of his monowheel, Roger and Ann Strang had breathed weakly, and decided between themselves that the boy should be scolded within an inch of his young life. And the fact that David maintained tenaciously that he had never swerved from the slow monowheel lane didn't bother his parents a bit. They were acquainted with another small-boy frailty. Small boys, on occasion, are inclined to fib.

But the second time, David was not fibbing. Roger Strang *saw* the *accident* the second time. He saw all the circumstances involved. And he realized, with horrible clarity, that someone, somehow, was trying to kill his son.

It had been late on a Saturday afternoon. The free week-ends that the Barrier Base engineers had once enjoyed to take their families for picnics "outside," or to rest and relax, were things of the past, for the work on the Barrier was reaching a critical stage, demanding more and more of the technicians, scientists and engineers engaged in its development. Already diplomatic relations with the Eurasian Combine were becoming more and more impossible; the Barrier *had* to be built, and quickly, or another more terrible New York City would be the result. Roger had never cleared from his mind the flaming picture of that night of horror, just five years before, when the mighty metropolis had burst into radioactive flame, to announce the beginning of the first Atomic War. The year 2078 was engraved in millions of minds as the year of the most horrible—and the shortest—war in all history, for an armistice had been signed not four days after the first bomb had been dropped. An armistice, but an uneasy peace, for neither of the great nations had really known what atomic war would be like until it had happened. And once upon them, they found that atomic war was not practical, for both mighty opponents would have been gutted in a matter of weeks. The armistice had stopped the bombs, but hostilities continued, until the combined scientific forces of one nation could succeed in preparing a defense.

That particular Saturday afternoon had been busy in the Main Labs on the Barrier Base. The problem of erecting a continent-long electronic Barrier to cover the coast of North America was a staggering proposition. Roger Strang was nearly finished and ready for home as dusk was falling. Leaving his work at the desk, he was slipping on his jacket when David came into the lab. He was small for twelve years, with tousled sand-brown hair standing up at odd angles about a sharp, intelligent face. "I came to get you, Daddy," he said.

Roger smiled. "You rode all the way down here—just to go home with me?"

"Maybe we could get some Icy-pops for supper on the way home," David remarked innocently.

Roger grinned broadly and slapped the boy on the back. "You'd sell your soul for an Icy-pop," he grinned.

The corridor was dark. The man and boy walked down to the elevator, and in a moment were swishing down to the dark and deserted lobby below.

David stepped first from the elevator when the men struck. One stood on either side of the door in the shadow. The boy screamed and reeled from the blow across the neck. Suddenly Roger heard the sharp pistol reports. David dropped with a groan, and Roger staggered against the wall from a powerful blow in the face. He shook his head groggily, catching a glimpse of the two men running through the door into the street below, as three or four people ran into the lobby, flushed out by the shots.

*

Roger shouted, pointing to the door, but the people were looking at the boy. Roger sank down beside his son, deft fingers loosening the blouse. The boy's small face was deathly white, fearful sobs choking his breath as he closed his eyes and shivered. Roger searched under his blouse, trying to find the bullet holes—and found to his chagrin that there weren't any bullet holes.

"Where did you feel the gun?"

David pointed vaguely at his lower ribs. "Right there," he said. "It hurt when they shoved the gun at me."

"But they couldn't have pulled the trigger, if the gun was pointed there—" He examined the unbroken skin on the boy's chest, fear tearing through his mind.

A Security man was there suddenly, asking about the accident, taking Roger's name, checking over the boy. Roger resented the tall man in the gray uniform, felt his temper rise at the slightly sarcastic tone of the questions. Finally the trooper stood up, shaking his head. "The boy must have been mistaken," he said. "Kids always have wild stories to tell. Whoever it was may have been after *somebody*, but they weren't aiming for the boy."

Roger scowled. "This boy is no liar," he snapped. "I saw them shoot—"

The trooper shrugged. "Well, he isn't hurt. Why don't you go on home?"

Roger helped the boy up, angrily. "You're not going to do anything about this?"

"What can I do? Nobody saw who the men were."

Roger grabbed the boy's hand, helped him to his feet, and turned angrily to the door. In the failing light outside the improbability of the attack struck through him strongly. He turned to the boy, his face dark. "David," he said evenly, "you wouldn't be making up stories about feeling that gun in your ribs, would you?"

David shook his head vigorously, eyes still wide with fear. "Honest, dad. I told you the truth."

"But they *couldn't* have shot you in the chest without breaking the skin—" He glanced down at the boy's blouse and jacket, and stopped suddenly, seeing the blackened holes in the ripped cloth. He stooped down and sniffed the holes suspiciously, and shivered suddenly in the cold evening air.

The burned holes smelled like gunpowder.

*

"Strang, you must have been wrong." The large man settled back in his chair, his graying hair smoothed over a bald spot. "Someone trying to kill you I could see—there's plenty of espionage going on, and you're doing important work here. But your boy!" The chief of the Barrier Base Security shook his head. "You must have been mistaken."

"But I *wasn't* mistaken!" Roger Strang sat forward in his chair, his hands gripping the arms until his knuckles were white. "I told you exactly what happened. They got him as he came off the elevator, and shot at him. Not at me, Morrel, at my son. They just clubbed me in the face to get me out of the way—"

"What sort of men?" Morrel's eyes were sharp.

Roger scowled, running his hand through his hair. "It was too dark to see. They wore hats and field jackets. The gun could be identified by ballistics. But they were *fast*, Morrel. They knew who they were looking for."

Morrel rose suddenly, his face impatient. "Strang," he said. "You've been here at the Base for quite awhile. Ever since a month after the war, isn't that right? August, 2078? Somewhere around there, I know. But you've been working hard. I think maybe a rest would do you some good—"

"Rest!" Roger exploded. "Look, man—I'm not joking. This isn't the first time. The boy had a monowheel accident three weeks ago, and he swore he was riding in a safe lane where he belonged. It looked like an accident then—now it looks like a murder attempt. The slugs from the gun *must* be in the building—embedded in the plasterwork somewhere. Surely you could try to trace the gun." He glared at the man's impassive face bitterly, "Or maybe you don't want to trace the gun—"

Morrel scowled. "I've already checked on it. The gun wasn't registered in the Base. Security has a check on every firearm within a fifty-mile range. The attackers must have been outsiders."

Roger's face flushed. "That's not true, Morrel," he said softly, "and you know it's not true."

Morrel shrugged. "Have it your own way," he said, indifferently. "Take a rest, Strang. Go home. Get some rest. And don't bother me with any more of your fairy tales." He turned suddenly on Roger. "And be careful what *you* do with guns, Strang. The only thing about this that I *do* know is that somebody shot a pistol off and scared hell out of your son. You were the only one around, as far as I know. I don't know your game, but you'd better be careful—"

*

Strang left Security Headquarters, and crossed across to the Labs, frustrated and angry. His mind spun over the accident—incredulous, but more incredulous that Morrel would practically laugh at him. He stopped by the Labs building to watch the workmen putting up a large electronic projector in one of the test yards. Work was going ahead. But so slowly.

Roger was aware of the tall thin man who had joined him before he looked around. Martin Drengo put a hand on his shoulder. "Been avoiding me lately?"

"Martin!" Roger Strang turned, his face lighting up. "No, not avoiding you—I've been so busy my own wife hasn't seen me in four days. How are things in Maintenance?"

9

INFINITE INTRUDER

The thin man smiled sadly. "How are things ever in Maintenance? First a railroad breaks down, then there's a steel strike, then some paymaster doesn't make a payroll—the war knocked things for a loop, Roger. Even now things are still loopy. And how are things in Production?"

Roger scowled. "Let's have some coffee," he said.

They sat in a back corner booth of the Base Dispensary as Roger told about David. Martin Drengo listened without interruption. He was a thin man from top to bottom, a shock of unruly black hair topping an almost cadaverous face, blue eyes large behind thick lenses. His whole body was like a skeleton, his fingers long and bony as he lit a cigarette. But the blue eyes were quick, and the nods warm and understanding. He listened, and then he said, "It couldn't have been an outsider?"

Roger shrugged. "Anything is possible. But why? Why go after a kid?"

Drengo hunched his shoulders forward. "I don't get it," he said. "David has done nothing to give him enemies." He drew on his cigarette. "What did Morrel have to say?"

"He laughed at me! Wouldn't even listen to me. Told me to go home and go to bed, that I was all wet. I tell you, Martin, I *saw* it! You know I wouldn't lie, you know I don't see things that don't happen."

"Yes," said Martin, glumly. "I believe you, all right. But I can't see why your son should be the target. You'd be more likely." He stood up, stretching his long legs. "Look, old boy. Take Morrel's advice, at least temporarily. Go home and get some sleep now; you're all worked up. I'll go in and talk to Morrel. Maybe I can handle that old buzzard better than you can."

Roger watched his friend amble down the aisle and out of the store. He felt better now that he had talked to Drengo. Smiling to himself, he finished off his coffee. Many a scrape he and Martin had seen through together. He remembered that night of horror when the bomb fell on the city, his miraculous rescue, the tall thin figure, reflecting the red glare from his glasses, forcing his way through the burning timbers of the building, tearing Roger's leg loose from the rubble covering it; the frightful struggle through the rubbish, fighting off fear-crazed mobs that sought to stop them, rob them, kill them. They had made the long trek together, Martin and he, the Evacuation Road down to Maryland, the Road of Horrors, lined with the rotting corpses of the dead and the soon-dead, the dreadful refuse of that horrible night. Martin Drengo had been a stout friend to Roger; he'd been with Martin the night he'd met Ann; took the ring from Martin's finger when they stood at the altar on their wedding day; shared with Martin his closest confidence.

Roger sighed and paid for the coffee. What to do? The boy was home now, recovering from the shock of the attack. Roger caught an out-bound tri-wheel, and sped down the busy thoroughfare toward his home. If Martin could talk to Morrel, and get something done, perhaps they could get a line. Somehow, perhaps they could trace the attackers. In the morning he'd see Martin again, and they could figure out a scheme.

But he didn't have a chance to see Martin again. For at 11:30 that night, the marauders struck again. For the third time.

*

Through his sleep he heard a door close down below, and sat bolt upright in bed, his heart pounding wildly. Only a tiny sound, the click of a closing door—

Ann was sitting up beside him, brown hair close around her head, her body tense. "Roger!" she whispered. "Did you hear something?"

Roger was out of bed, bounding across the room, into the hall. Blood pounded in his ears as he rushed to David's room, stopped short before the open door.

The shots rang out like whip cracks, and he saw the yellow flame from the guns. There were two men in the dark room, standing at the bed where the boy lay rolled into a terrified knot. The guns cracked again and again, ripping the bedding, bursting the pillow into a shower of feathers, tearing the boy's pajamas from his thin body, a dozen blazing shots—

Roger let out a strangled cry, grabbed one of the men by the throat, in a savage effort to stop the murderous pistols. The other man caught him a coarse blow behind the ear, and he staggered hard against the wall. Dully he heard the door slam, heavy footsteps down the corridor, running down the stairs.

He struggled feebly to his feet, glancing at the still form on the bed. Choking back a sob he staggered down the hall, shouting to Ann as he went down the stairs, redoubling his speed as he heard the purr of autojets in the driveway. In a moment he was in his own car, frantically stamping on the starter. It started immediately, the motor booming, and the powerful jet engines forced the heavy car ahead dangerously, taking the corner on two of its three wheels. He knew that Ann would call Security, and he raced to gain on the tail lights that were disappearing down the winding residential road to the main highway. Throwing caution to the winds, Roger swerved the car across a front lawn, down between two houses, into an alley, and through another driveway, gaining three blocks. Ahead, at the junction with the main Base highway he saw the long black autojet turn right.

*

Roger snaked into traffic on the highway and bore down on the black car. Traffic was light because of the late hour, but the patrol was on the road and might stop him instead of the killers. The other car was traveling at top speed, swerving around the slower cars. Roger gained slowly. He fingered the spotlight, preparing to snap it in the driver's eyes. Taking a curve at 90, he crept up alongside the black car as he heard the siren of a patrol car behind him. Cursing, he edged over on the black car, snapped the spotlight full in the face of the driver—

The screaming siren forced him off the road, and he braked hard, his hands trembling. A patrolman came over to the car, gun drawn. He took a quick look at Roger, and his face tightened. "Mr. Strang," he said sharply. "We've been looking for you. You're wanted at Security."

"That car," Roger started weakly. "You've got to stop that car I was chasing—"

"Never mind that car," the patrolman snarled. "It's you they want. Hop out. We'll go in the patrol car."

"You've got to stop them—"

The patrolman fingered his gun. "Security wants to talk to you, Mr. Strang. Hop out."

Roger moved dazedly from his car. He didn't question the patrolman; he hardly even heard him. His mind raced in a welter of confusion, trying desperately to refute the brilliant picture in his mind from that split-second that the spotlight had rested on the driver of the black car, trying to fit the impossible pieces into their places. For the second man in the black autojet had been John Morrel, chief of Barrier Base Security, and the driver had been Martin Drengo—

*

The man at the desk was a stranger to Roger Strang. He was an elderly man, stooped, with graying hair and a small clipped mustache that seemed to stick out like antennae. He watched Roger impassively with steel gray eyes, motioning him to a chair.

"You led us a merry chase," he said flatly, his voice brittle. "A very merry chase. The alarm went out for you almost an hour ago."

Strang's cheeks were red with anger. "My son was shot tonight. I was trying to follow the killers—"

"Killers?" The man raised his eyebrows.

"Yes, killers!" Roger snapped. "Do I have to draw you a picture? They shot my son down in his bed."

INFINITE INTRUDER

The gray-haired man stared at him for a long time. "Well," he said finally in a baffled tone. "Now I've heard everything."

It was Roger's turn to stare. "Can't you understand what I've said? *My son was murdered.*"

The gray-haired man flipped a pencil down on the desk impatiently. "Mr. Strang," he said elaborately. "My name is Whitman. I flew down here from Washington tonight, after being called from my bed by the commanding officer of this base. I am the National Chief of the Federal Bureau of Security, Mr. Strang, and I am not interested in fairy tales. I would like you to come off it now, and answer some questions for me. And I don't want double-talk. I want answers. Do I make myself quite clear?"

Roger stared at him, finally nodded his head. "Quite," he said sourly.

Whitman hunched forward in his chair. "Mr. Strang, how long have you been working in the Barrier Base?"

"Five years. Ever since the bombing of New York."

Whitman nodded. "Oh, yes. The bombing of New York." He looked sharply at Roger. "And how old are you, Mr. Strang?"

Roger looked up, surprised. "Thirty-two, of course. You have my records. Why are you asking?"

The gray-haired man lit a cigarette. "Yes, we have your records," he said offhandedly. "Very interesting records, quite normal, quite in order. Nothing out of the ordinary." He stood up and looked out on the dark street. "Just one thing wrong with your records, Mr. Strang. They aren't true."

Roger stared. "This is ridiculous," he blurted. "What do you mean, they aren't true?"

Whitman took a deep breath, and pulled a sheet of paper out of a sheaf on his desk. "It says here," he said, "that you are Roger Strang, and that you were born in Indianola, Iowa, on the fourteenth of June, 2051. That your father was Jason Strang, born 11 August, 2023, in Chicago, Illinois. That you lived in Indianola until you were twelve, when your father moved to New York City, and was employed with the North American Electronics Laboratories. That you entered International Polytechnic Institute at the age of 21, studying physics and electronics, and graduated in June 2075 with the degree of Bachelor of Electronics. That you did further work, taking a Masters and Doctorate in Electronics at Polytech in 2077."

Whitman took a deep breath. "That's what it says here. A very ordinary record. But there is no record there of your birth in Indianola, Iowa, in 2051 or any other time. There is no record there of your father, the alleged Jason Strang, nor in Chicago. No one by the name of Jason Strang was ever employed by North American Electronics. No one by the name of Roger Strang ever attended Polytech." Whitman watched him with cold eyes. "To the best of our knowledge, and according to all available records, *there never was anyone named Roger Strang until after the bombing of New York.*"

Roger sat stock still, his mind racing. "This is silly," he said finally. "Perfectly idiotic. Those schools *must* have records—"

Whitman's face was tight. "They do have records. Complete records. But the name of Roger Strang is curiously missing from the roster of graduates in 2075. Or any other year." He snubbed his cigarette angrily. "I wish you would tell me, and save us both much unpleasantness. *Just who are you, Mr. Strang, and where do you come from?*"

Strang stared at the man, his pulse pounding in his head. Filtering into his mind was a vast confusion, some phrase, some word, some nebulous doubt that frightened him, made him almost believe that gray-haired man in the chair before him. He took a deep breath, clearing his mind of the nagging doubt. "Look here," he said, exasperated. "When I was drafted for the Barrier Base, they checked for my origin, for my education and credentials. If they had been false, I'd have been snapped up right then. Probably shot—they were shooting people for chewing their fingernails in those days. I wouldn't have stood a chance."

INFINITE INTRUDER

Whitman nodded his head vigorously. "Exactly!" he snapped. "You *should* have been picked up. But you weren't even suspected until we did a little checking after that accident in the Labs building yesterday. Somehow, false credentials got through for you. Security does not like false credentials. I don't know how you did it, but you did. I want to know how."

"But, I tell you—" Roger stood up, fear suddenly growing in his mind. He lit a cigarette, took two nervous puffs, and set it down, forgotten, on the ash-tray. "I have a wife," he said shakily. "I married her in New York City. We had a son, born in a hospital in New York City. He went to school there. Surely there must be some kind of record—"

Whitman smiled grimly, almost mockingly. "Good old New York City," he snarled. "Married there, you say? Wonderful! Son born there? In the one city in the country where that information *can never be checked*. That's very convenient, Mr. Strang. Or whoever you are. I think you'd better talk."

Roger snubbed out the cigarette viciously. "My son," he said after a long pause. "He was murdered tonight. Shot down in his bed—"

The Security Chief's face went white. "Garbage!" he snapped. "What kind of a fool do you think I am, Strang? Your son murdered—bah! When the alarm went out for you I personally drove to your home. Oddly enough this wife of yours wasn't at home, but your son was. Nice little chap. He made us some coffee, and explained that he didn't know where his parents were, because he'd been asleep all night. Quietly asleep in his bed—"

The words were clipped out, and rang in Roger's ears, incredibly. His hand shook violently as he puffed his cigarette, burning his fingers on the short butt. "I don't believe it," he muttered hollowly. "I saw it happen—"

Whitman sneered. "Are you going to talk or not?"

Roger looked up helplessly. "I don't—know—" he said, weakly. "I don't know."

The Security Chief threw up his hands in disgust. "Then we'll do it the hard way," he grated. Flipping an intercom switch, his voice snapped out cold in the still room. "Send in Psych squad," he growled. "We've got a job to do—"

*

Roger Strang lay back on the small bunk, his nerves yammering from the steady barrage, lights still flickering green and red in his eyes. His body was limp, his mind functioning slowly, sluggishly. His eyelids were still heavy from the drugs, his wrists and forehead burning and sore where the electrodes had been attached. His muscles hardly responded when he tried to move, his strength completely gone—washed out. He simply lay there, his shallow breathing returning to him from the dark stone walls.

The inquisition had been savage. The hot lights, the smooth-faced men firing questions, over and over, the drugs, the curious sensation of mouthing nonsense, of hearing his voice rambling on crazily, yet being unable in any way to control it; the hypnotic effect of Whitman's soft voice, the glitter in his steel-gray eyes, and the questions, questions, questions. The lie detector had been going by his side, jerking insanely at his answers, every time the same answers, every time setting the needle into wild gyrations. And finally the foggy, indistinct memory of Whitman mopping his forehead and stamping savagely on a cigarette, and muttering desperately, "It's no use! Lies! Nothing but lies, lies, lies! He *couldn't* be lying under this treatment, but he is. *And he knows he is!*"

Lies? Roger stretched his heavy limbs, his mind struggling up into a tardy rejection. Not lies! He hadn't lied—he had been answering the truth to the questions. He couldn't have been lying, for the answers were there, clear in his memory. And yet—the same nagging doubt crept through, the same feeling that had plagued him throughout the inquisition, the nagging, haunting, horrible conviction, somewhere in the depths of his numb brain that he *was* lying! Something was missing somewhere, some vast gap in his knowledge, something of which he simply was not aware. The incredible turnabout of Martin Drengo, the attack on David, who was killed, but somehow was not dead. He *had* to be lying—

But how could he lie, and still know that he was not lying? His sluggish mind wrestled, trying to choke back the incredible doubt. Somewhere in the morass, the picture of Martin Drengo came through—Drengo, the traitor, who was trying to kill his son—but the conviction swept through again, overpowering, the certain knowledge that Drengo was *not* a traitor, that he must trust Drengo. Drengo was his friend, his stalwart—

HIS AGENT!

Strang sat bolt upright on the cot, his head spinning. The thought had broken through crystal clear in the darkness, revealed itself for the briefest instant, then swirled down again into the foggy gulf. Agent? Why should he have an agent? What purpose? Frantically he scanned his memory for Drengo, down along the dark channels, searching. Drengo had come through the fire, into the burning building, carried him like a child through the flames into safety. Drengo had been best man at his wedding—but he'd been married before the bombing of the city. *Or had he?* Where did Drengo fit in? Was the fire the first time he had seen Drengo?

Something deep in his mind forced its way through, saying NO! YOU HAVE KNOWN HIM ALL YOUR LIFE! Roger fought it back, frantically. Never! Back in Iowa there had been no Drengo. Nor in Chicago. Nor in New York. He hadn't even known him in—IN NEW ALBANY!

*

Roger Strang was on his feet, shaking, cold fear running through his body, his nerves screaming. Had they ruined his mind? He couldn't think straight any more. Telling him things that weren't true, forcing lies into his mind—frightening him with the horrible conviction that his mind was really helpless, full of false data. What had happened to him? Where had the thought of "New Albany" come from? He shivered, now thoroughly frightened. There wasn't any "New Albany." Nowhere in the world. There just *wasn't* any such place.

Could he have two memories? Conflicting memories?

He walked shakily to the door, peered through the small peephole. In the morning they would try again, they had said. He shuddered, terribly afraid. He had felt his mind cracking under the last questioning; another would drive him completely insane. But Drengo would have the answers. Why had he shot little Davey? How did that fit in? Was this false-credential business part of some stupendous scheme against him? Impossible! But what else? He knew with sudden certain conviction that he must see Martin Drengo, immediately, before they questioned him again, before the fear and uncertainty drove him out of his mind. He called tentatively through the peephole, half-hoping to catch a guard's attention. And the call echoed through silent halls.

And then he heard Ann's voice, clear, cool, sharp in the prison darkness. Roger whirled, fear choking the shouts still ringing in his ears, gaped at the woman who stood in his cell—

She was lovelier than he had ever seen her, her tiny body clothed in a glowing fabric which clung to every curve, accenting her trim figure, her slender hips. Brown hair wreathed her lovely face, and Roger choked as the deep longing for her welled up in his throat. Speechlessly he took her in his arms, holding her close, burying his face in her hair, sobbing in joy and relief. And then he saw the glowing circle behind her, casting its eerie light into the far corners of the dark cell. In fiery greenness the ring shimmered in an aurora of violent power, but Ann paid no attention to it. She stepped back and smiled at him, her eyes bright. "Don't be frightened," she said softly, "and don't make any noise. I'm here to help you."

"But where did you come from?" The question forced itself out in a sort of strangled gasp.

INFINITE INTRUDER

"We have—means of going where we want to. And we want you to come with us." She pointed at the glowing ring. "We want to take you back to the time-area from which you came."

Roger goggled at her, confusion welling strong into his mind again. "Ann," he said weakly. "What kind of trick is this?"

She smiled again. "No trick," she said. "Don't ask questions, darling. I know you're confused, but there isn't much time. You'll just have to do what I say right now." She turned to the glowing ring. "We just step through here. Be careful that you don't touch the substance of the portal going through."

Roger Strang approached the glowing ring curiously, peered through, blinked, peered again. It was like staring at an inscrutable flat-black surface in the shadow. No light reflected through it; nothing could be seen. He heard a faint whining as he stood close to the ring, and he looked up at Ann, his eyes wide. "You can't see through it!" he exclaimed.

Ann was crouching on the floor near a small metallic box, gently turning knobs, checking the dial reading against a small chronometer on her wrist. "Steady, darling," she said. "Just follow me, carefully, and don't be afraid. We're going back home—to the time-area where we belong. You and I. I know—you don't remember. And you'll be puzzled, and confused, because the memory substitution job was very thorough. But you'll remember Martin Drengo, and John Morrel, and me. And I was your wife there, too—Are you ready?"

Roger stared at the ring for a moment. "Where are we going?" he asked. "How far ahead? Or behind—?"

"Ahead," she said. "Eighty years ahead—as far as we can go. That will bring us to the present time, the *real* present time, as far as we, and you, are concerned."

She turned abruptly, and stepped through the ring, and vanished as effectively as if she had disintegrated into vapor. Roger felt fear catch at his throat; then he followed her through.

They were standing in a ruins. The cell was gone, the prison, the Barrier Base. The dark sky above was bespeckled with a myriad of stars, and a cool night breeze swept over Roger's cheek. Far in the distance a low rumble came to his ears. "Sounds like a storm coming," he muttered to Ann, pulling his jacket closer around him.

"No storm," she said grimly. "Look!" She pointed a finger toward the northern horizon. Brazen against the blackness the yellow-orange of fire was rising, great spurts of multi-colored flames licking at the horizon. The rumble became a drone, a roar. Ann grasped Roger's arm and pulled him down to cover in the rubble as the invisible squadron swished across the sky, trailing jet streams of horrid orange behind them. Then to the south, in the direction of the flight, the drone of the engines gave way to the hollow boom-booming of bombing, and the southern horizon flared. Then, as suddenly as it had appeared, the rumble died away, leaving the flames licking the sky to the north and south.

Roger shivered. "War," he said. "Eurasia?"

She shook her head. "If only it were. There is no Eurasia now. The dictator took care of that. Nothing but gutted holes, and rubble." She stood up, helping Roger to his feet. Together they filed through the rubbish down to a roadway. Ann dialed a small wrist radio; in a few moments, out of the dark sky, the dim-out lights of a small 'copter came into view, and the machine settled delicately to the road. Two strange men were inside; they saluted Ann, and helped Roger aboard. Swiftly they clamped down the hatch tight, and the ship rose again silently into the air.

"Where are we going?" asked Roger Strang.

"We have a headquarters. Our data must be checked first. We can't reach a decision without checking. Then we can talk."

The 'copter swung high over the blazing inferno of a city far below. Strang glanced from the window, eyes widening at the holocaust. The crater holes were mammoth, huge spires of living flame rising to the sky, leaving mushroom columns of gray-black smoke that glowed an evil red from the furnace on the ground. "Not Eurasia?" Roger asked suddenly, his mind twisting in amazement. "But who? This is America, isn't it?"

"Yes. This is America. There is no Eurasia now. Soon there may not be an America. Nor even an Earth."

Roger looked up at Ann, eyes wide. "But those jet-planes—the bombing—*who is doing the bombing?*"

Ann Strang stared down at the sullen red fires of the city for a moment, her quiet eyes sad. "Those are Martian planes," she said.

*

The 'copter settled silently down into the heart of the city, glowing red from the flames and bombing. They hovered over the shining Palace, still tall, and superb, and intact, gleaming like a blood-streaked jewel in the glowing night. The 'copter settled on the roof of a low building across a large courtyard from the glittering Palace. Ann Strang stepped out, and motioned Roger to follow down a shaft and stairway into a small room below. She knocked at a door, and a strange man dressed in the curious glowing fabric opened it. His face lit up in a smile.

"Roger!" he cried. "We were afraid we couldn't locate you. We weren't expecting the Security to meddle. Someone got suspicious, somewhere, and began checking your references from their sources—and of course they were false. We were lucky to get you back at all, after Security got you." He clapped Roger on the back, and led him into the room.

John Morrel and Martin Drengo were standing near the rounded window, their faces thrown into grotesque relief against the red-orange glow outside. They turned and saluted, and Roger almost cried out, his mind spinning, a thousand questions cutting into his consciousness, demanding answers. But quite suddenly he was feeling a new power, a new effectiveness in his thinking, in his activity. He turned to Martin Drengo, his eyes questioning but no longer afraid. "What year is this?" he asked.

ALAN E. NOURSE

"This is 2165. March, 2165, and you're in New Albany, in the United States of North America. This is the city where you were born, the city you loved—and look at it!"

Roger walked to the window. The court below was full of people now, ragged people, some of them screaming, a disconsolate muttering rising from a thousand throats—burned people, mangled people. They milled about the mammoth courtyard before the glorious Palace, aimlessly, mindlessly. Far down the avenue leading from the Palace Roger could see the people evacuating the city, a long, desolate line of people, strange autos, carts, even animals, running down the broad avenue to escape from the flaming city.

"We're not in danger here," said Drengo, at his elbow. "No fire nor bomb can reach us here—that is the result of your mighty Atlantic Coast Barrier. Nothing more. It never was perfected in time, before the great Eastern Invasion and the second Atomic War. That was due to occur three years after the time-area where we visited. We were trying to stem it, to turn it aside. We don't know yet whether we succeeded or not."

He turned to the tall man standing at the door. "Markson, all the calculations are prepared. The Calc is evaluating the data against the Equation now, figuring all the variables. If our work did any good, we should know it soon." He sighed and pointed to the Palace. "But our fine Dictator is still alive, and the attack on Mars should be starting any minute—If we didn't succeed, nothing in all Time will stop him."

Roger lit a cigarette, his eyes questioning Drengo. "Dictator?"

Drengo sat down and stretched his legs. "The Dictator appeared four years ago, a nobody, a man from the masses of people on the planet. He rose into public favor like a sky-rocket, a remarkable man, an amazing man—a man who could talk to you, and control your thoughts in a single interview. There has never been a man with such personal magnetism and power, Roger, in all the history of Earth. A

23

man who raised himself from nothing into absolute Dictatorship, and has handled the world according to his whim ever since.

"He is only a young man, Roger, just 32 years of age, but an irresistible man who can win anything from anybody. He writhed into the presidency first, and then deliberately set about rearranging the government to suit himself. And the people let him get away with it, followed him like sheep. And then he was Dictator, and he began turning the social and economic balance of the planet into a whirlwind. And then came Mars."

Martin stretched again, and lit a cigarette, his thin face grave in the darkened room. "The first landing was thirty years ago, and the possibilities for rich and peaceful commerce between Earth and Mars were clear from the first. Mars had what Earth lacked: the true civilization, the polished culture, the lasting socio-economic balance, the permanent peace. Mars could have taught us so much. She could have guided us out of the mire of war and hatred that we have been wallowing in for centuries. But the Dictator put an end to those possibilities." Drengo shrugged. "He was convinced that the Martians were weak, backward, decadent. He saw their uranium, their gold, their jewelry, their labor—and started on a vast impossible imperialism. If he had had his way, he would have stripped the planet in three years, but the Martians fought against us, turned from peace to suspicion, and finally to open revolt. And the Dictator could not see. He mobilized Earth for total war against Mars, draining our resources, decimating our population, building rockets, bombs, guns—" He stopped for a moment, breathing deeply. "But the Dictator didn't know what he was doing. He had never been on Mars. He has never seen Martians. He had no idea what they think, what they are capable of doing. He doesn't know what we know—that the Martians will win. He doesn't realize that the Martians can carry out a war for years without shaking their economy one iota, while he has drained our planet to such a degree that a war of more than two or three months will break us in half. He doesn't know that Mars can win, and that the Earth can't—"

Roger walked across the room, thoughtfully, his mind fitting pieces into place. "But where do I come in? David—Ann—I don't understand—"

Drengo looked Roger straight in the eye. "The Dictator's name," he said, "is Farrel Strang."

Roger stopped still. "Strang?" he echoed.

"Your son, Roger. Yours and Ann's."

"But—you said the Dictator was only 32—" Roger trailed off, regarding Ann in amazement.

Martin smiled. "People don't grow old so quickly nowadays," he said. "You are 57 years old, Roger. Ann is 53." He leaned back in his chair, his gaunt smile fading. "The Dictator has not been without opposition. You, his parents, opposed him at the very start, and he cast you off. People wiser than the crowds were able to rebuff his powerful personal appeal, to see through the robe of glory he had wrapped around himself. He has opposition, but he has built himself an impregnable fortress, and dealt swift death to any persons suspected of treason. A few have escaped—scientists, technologists, sociologists, physicists. The work of one group of men gave us a weapon which we hoped to use to destroy the Dictator. We found a way to move back in Time. We could leave the normal time-stream and move to any area of past time. So four of us went back, searching for the core of the economic and social upheaval on Earth, and trying to destroy the Dictator before he was born. Given Time travel, it should have been possible. So we went back—myself, John Morrel, Ann Strang, and you."

Roger shook his head, a horrible thought forming in his mind. "You were trying to kill David—my son—" he stopped short. "David *couldn't* have been my son!" He whirled on Martin Drengo. "*Who was that boy?*"

INFINITE INTRUDER

Martin looked away then, his face white. "The boy was your father," he said.

*

The drone of the jet bombers came again, whining into the still room. Roger Strang stood very still, staring at the gaunt man. Slowly the puzzle was beginning to fit together, and horror filtered into his mind. "My father—" he said. "Only twelve years old, but he was to be my father." He stared helplessly at the group in the room. "You were trying—to kill him!"

Martin Drengo stood up, his lean face grave. "We were faced with a terrific problem. Once we returned to a time-area, we had no way of knowing to what extent we could effect people and events that had already happened. We had to go back, to fit in, somehow, in an area where we never had been, to *make* things happen that had never happened before. We knew that if there was any way of doing it, we had to destroy Farrel Strang. But the patterns of history which had allowed him to rise had to be altered, too; destroying the man would not have been enough. So we tried to destroy him in the time-area where the leading time-patterns of *our* time had been formed. We had to kill his grandfather."

Roger shivered. "But if you had killed David—what would have happened *to me?*"

"Presumably the same thing that would have happened to the Dictator. In theory, *if we had succeeded* in killing your father, David, both you and the Dictator would have ceased to exist." Drengo took a deep breath. "The idea was yours, Roger. You knew the terrible damage your son was doing as Dictator. It was a last resort, and Ann and John and I pleaded with you to reconsider. But it was the obvious step."

Ann walked over to Roger, her face pale. "You insisted, Roger. So we did what we could to make it easy. We used the Dictator's favorite trick—a psycho-purge—to clear your mind of all conscious and subconscious memory of your true origin and environment, replacing it with a history and memory of the past-time area where we were going. We chose the contact-time carefully, so that we appeared in New York in the confusion of the bombing of 2078, making sure that your records would stand up under all but the closest examination. From then on, when Martin carried you out from the fire, you stored your own memory of that time-area and became a legitimate member of that society."

"But how could we pose as David's *parents*, if he was my father?"

Ann smiled. "Both David's parents were killed in the New York bombing; we knew that David survived, and we knew where he could be found. There was a close physical resemblance between you and the boy, though actually the resemblance was backwards, and he accepted you as a foster-father without question. With you equipped with a complete memory of your marriage to me in that time, of David's birth, and of your own history before and after the bombing of New York, you fit in well and played the part to perfection. Also, you acted as a control, to guide us, since you had no conscious knowledge beyond that time-area. Martin and Morrel were to be the assassins, the Intruders, and I was to keep tabs on you—"

"And the success of the attempt?"

Ann's face fell. "We don't know yet. We don't know what we accomplished, whether we stemmed the war or not—"

The tall man who had stepped into the room moved forward and threw a sheaf of papers on the floor, his face heavy with anger, his voice hoarse. "Yes, I'm afraid we do know," he said bitterly.

Martin Drengo whirled on him, his face white. "What do you mean, Markson?"

The tall man sank down in a chair tiredly. "We've lost, Martin. We don't need these calculations to tell. The word was just broadcast on the telecast. Farrel Strang's armada has just begun its attack on Mars—"

*

INFINITE INTRUDER

For a moment the distant bombing was the only sound in the room. Then Martin Drengo said, "So he gave the order. And we've lost."

"We only had a theory to work on," said Morrel, staring gloomily at the curved window. "A theory and an equation. The theory said that a man returning through time could alter the social and technological trends of the people and times to which he returned, in order to change history that was already past. The theory said that if we could turn the social patterns and technological trends just slightly away from what they were, we could alter the entire makeup of society in our own time. And the Equation was the tool, the final check on any change. The Equation which evaluates the sum of social, psychological and energy factors in any situation, any city or nation or human society. The Equation has been proven, checked time and time again, but the theory didn't fit it. The theory was wrong."

Roger Strang sat up, suddenly alert. "That boy," he said, his voice sharp. "You nearly made a sieve of him, trying to shoot him. Why didn't he die?"

"Because he was on a high-order variable. Picture it this way: From any point in time, the possible future occurrences could be seen as vectors, an infinite number of possible vectors. Every activity that makes an alteration, or has any broad effect on the future is a high-order variable, but many activities have no grave implications for future time, and could be considered unimportant, or low-order variables. If a man turns a corner and sees something that stimulates him into writing a world-shaking manifesto, the high-order variable would have started when he decided to turn the corner instead of going the other way. But if he took one way home instead of another, and nothing of importance occurred as a result of the decision, a low-order variable would be set up.

"We found that the theory of alterations held quite well, for low-order variables. Wherever we appeared, whatever we did, we set up a definite friction in the normal time-stream, a distortion, like pulling a taut rubber band out. And we could produce changes—on low-order variables. But the elasticity of the distortion was so great as to warp the change back into the time-stream without causing any lasting alteration. When it came to high-order changes, *we simply couldn't make any.* We tried putting wrong data into the machines that were calculating specifications for the Barrier, and the false data went in, but the answers that came out were answers that *should* have appeared with the *right* data. We tried to commit a murder, to kill David Strang, and try as we would we couldn't do it. Because it would have altered a high-order variable, and they simply *wouldn't be altered!*"

"But you, Morrel," Roger exclaimed. "How about you? You were top man in the Barrier Base Security office. You must have made an impression."

Morrel smiled tiredly. "I really thought I had, time after time. I would start off a series of circumstances that should have had a grave alterative effect, and it would look for awhile as if a long-range change was going to be affected—and then it would straighten itself out again, with no important change occurring. It was maddening. We worked for five years trying to make even a small alteration—and brought back our data—" He pointed to the papers on the floor. "There are the calculations, applied on the Equation. Meaningless. We accomplished nothing. And the Dictator is still there."

Drengo slumped in his chair. "And he's started the war. The real attack. This bombardment outside is nothing. There are fifteen squadrons of space-destroyers already unloading atomic bombs on the surface of Mars, and that's the end, for us. Farrel Strang has started a war he can never finish—"

Roger Strang turned sharply to Drengo. "This Dictator," he said. "Where is he? Why can't he be reached now, and destroyed?"

"The Barrier. He can't be touched in the Palace. He has all his offices there, all his controls, and he won't let anyone in since the attempted assassination three months ago. He's safe there, and we can't touch him."

Roger scowled at the control panel on the wall. "How does this time-portal work?" he asked. "You say it can take us back—*why not forward?*"

"No good. The nature of Time itself makes that impossible. At the present instant of Time, everything that has happened has happened. The three-dimensional world in which we live has passed through the fourth temporal dimension, and nothing can alter it. But at this instant there are an infinite number of things that could happen next. The future is an infinite series of variables, and there's no conceivable way to predict which variable will actually be true."

Roger Strang sat up straight, staring at Drengo. "Will that portal work both ways?" he asked tensely.

Drengo stared at him blankly. "You mean, can it be reverse-wired? I suppose so. But—anyone trying to move into the future would necessarily become an *infinity* of people—he couldn't maintain his identity, because he'd have to have a body in every one of an infinite number of places he might be—"

"—*until the normal time stream caught up with him in the future!* And then he'd be in whatever place he fit!" Roger's voice rose excitedly. "Martin, can't you see the implications? Send me ahead—just a little ahead, an hour or so—and let me go into the Palace. If I moved my consciousness to the place where the Palace should be, where the Dictator should be, then when normal time caught up with me, *I could kill him!*"

Drengo was on his feet, staring at Roger with rising excitement. Suddenly he glanced at his watch. "By God!" he muttered. "*Maybe you could—*"

*

Blackness.

He had no body, no form. There was no light, no shape, nothing but eternal, dismal, unbroken blackness. This was the Void, the place

30

where time had not yet come. Roger Strang shuddered, and felt the cold chill of the blackness creep into his marrow. He had to move. He wanted to move, to find the right place, moving with the infinity of possible bodies. A stream of consciousness was all he could grasp, for the blackness enclosed everything. A sort of death, but he knew he was not dead. Blackness was around him, and in him, and through him.

He could feel the timelessness, the total absence of anything. Suddenly he felt the loneliness, for he knew there was no going back. He had to transfer his consciousness, his mind, to the place where the Dictator was, hoping against hope that he could find the place before time caught him wedged in the substance of the stone walls of the Palace. He reached the place that *should* be right, and waited—

And waited. There was no time in this place, and he had to wait for the normal time stream. The blackness worked at his mind, filling him with fear, choking him, making him want to scream in frightened agony—waiting—

And suddenly, abruptly, he was standing in a brightly lighted room. The arched dome over his head sparkled with jewels, and through paneled windows the red glow of the city's fires flickered grimly. *He was in the Palace!*

He looked about swiftly, and crossed the room toward a huge door. In an instant he had thrown it open. The bright lights of the office nearly blinded him, and the man behind the desk rose angrily, caught Roger's eye full--

Roger gasped, his eyes widening. For a moment he thought he was staring into a mirror. For the man behind the desk, clothed in a rich glowing tunic was a living image of—*himself!*

The Dictator's face opened into startled surprise and fear as he recognized Roger, and a frightened cry came from his lips. There was no one else in the room, but his eyes ran swiftly to the visiphone. With careful precision Roger Strang brought the heat-pistol to eye level, and pulled the trigger. Farrel Strang crumpled slowly from the knees, a black hole scorched in his chest.

Roger ran to the fallen man, stared into his face incredulously. His son—and himself, as alike as twin dolls, for all the age difference. Drengo's words rose in Roger's mind: "Medicine is advanced, you know. People don't grow old so soon these days—"

Swiftly Roger slipped from his clothes, an impossibly bold idea translating itself into rapid action. He stripped the glowing tunic from the man's flaccid body, and slipped his arms into the sleeves, pulling the cape in close to cover the burned spot.

He heard a knock on the door. Frantically he forced the body under the heavy desk, and sat down in the chair behind it, eyes wide with fear. "Come in," he croaked.

A young deputy stepped through the door, approached the desk deferentially. "The first reports, sir," he said, looking straight at Roger. Not a flicker of suspicion crossed his face. "The attack is progressing as expected."

"Turn all reports over to my private teletype," Roger snapped. The man saluted. "Immediately, sir!" He turned and left the room, closing the door behind him.

Roger panted, closing his eyes in relief. He could pass! Turning to the file, he examined the detailed plans for the Martian attack; the numbers of ships, the squadron leaders, the zero hours—then he was at the teletype keyboard, passing on the message of peace, the message to stop the War with Mars, to make an armistice; ALL SQUADRONS AND SHIPS ATTENTION: CEASE AND DESIST IN ATTACK PLANS: RETURN TO TERRA IMMEDIATELY: BY ORDER OF FARREL STRANG.

Wildly he tore into the files, ripping out budget reports, stabilization plans, battle plans, evacuation plans. It would be simple to dispose of the Dictator's body as that of an imposter, an assassin—and simply take control himself in Farrel's place. They would carry on with *his* plans, *his* direction. And an era of peace, and stability and rich commerce would commence at long last. The sheaf of papers grew larger and larger as Roger emptied out the files: plans of war, plans of conquest, of slavery—he aimed the heat-pistol at the pile, saw it spring into yellow flame, and circle up to the vaulted ceiling in blue smoke.

*

And then he sat down, panting, and flipped the visiphone switch. "Send one man, unarmed, to the building across the courtyard. Have him bring Martin Drengo to me."

The deputy's eyes widened on the screen. "Unarmed, sir?"

"Unarmed," Roger repeated. "By order of your Dictator."